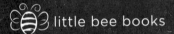 little bee books

An imprint of Bonnier Publishing USA
251 Park Avenue South, New York, NY 10010
Copyright © 2018 by Bonnier Publishing USA
All rights reserved, including the right of reproduction in whole or in part in any form.
Little Bee Books is a trademark of Bonnier Publishing USA, and associated colophon is a trademark of Bonnier Publishing USA.

Names: Newton, A. I., author. | Sarkar, Anjan, illustrator.
Title: Alien scout / A. I. Newton; Anjan Sarkar.
Description: First edition. | New York, NY: Little Bee Books, [2018]
Series: The alien next door; book 3 | Summary: Harris invites Zeke to join him for a weekend at Beaver Scout Camp, but Zeke needs help understanding the activities and hiding his alien abilities from the other campers. | Identifiers: LCCN 2017057014 | Subjects: | CYAC: Extraterrestrial beings—Fiction. | Ability—Fiction. | Friendship—Fiction. | Camping—Fiction. | Scouting (Youth activity)—Fiction. | Science fiction. | BISAC: JUVENILE FICTION / Readers / Chapter Books. | JUVENILE FICTION / Science Fiction. | JUVENILE FICTION / Action & Adventure / General. | Classification: LCC PZ7.1.N498 Ald 2018 | DDC [Fic]—dc23 | LC record available at https://lccn.loc.gov/2017057014

Printed in the United States of America LAK 0318
ISBN 978-1-4998-0581-9 (hardcover)
First Edition 10 9 8 7 6 5 4 3 2 1
ISBN 978-1-4998-0580-2 (paperback)
First Edition 10 9 8 7 6 5 4 3 2 1
ISBN 978-1-4998-0582-6 (ebook)

littlebeebooks.com
bonnierpublishingusa.com

THE ALIEN NEXT DOOR

ALIEN SCOUT

by A. I. Newton
illustrated by Anjan Sarkar

little bee books

TABLE OF CONTENTS

1 — A FRIEND'S SECRET

HARRIS WALKER AND HIS FRIEND ZEKE were sprawled out on the floor of Harris's bedroom, reading comic books. Harris loved showing off his collection.

"Now this one is called *Invaders From Beyond*," Harris said. "It's about these aliens from another dimension who can travel through time and shoot power beams from their eyes that can blow up entire mountains."

Zeke looked at his friend and laughed.

"You don't really believe all this stuff is true, do you?" he asked.

Harris laughed, too.

"Well, *you* can do some pretty amazing things, can't you?" he asked.

A lot had changed in the friendship between the two next-door neighbors since Zeke finally admitted the truth to Harris—Zeke was an alien from the planet Tragas!

"Yeah, but not *that* amazing," said Zeke. "Traveling through time and blowing up mountains is a bit beyond my skills."

"Okay, so what *can* you actually do?" Harris asked. "I mean, I know you can float, you can project what you see in your head onto screens, and you can heat stuff up with your hands."

"Let's see," Zeke said. "I can also move objects with my mind."

The next page in the comic book page turned over all by itself, revealing a picture of an alien lifting an entire building with one hand.

"Well, I definitely can't do *that*!" Zeke said.

Both boys laughed.

The next morning, Harris sat on the school bus next to Zeke.

"I just found out that I'm going on a camping weekend with the Beaver Scouts," Harris said excitedly.

"Beaver Scouts?" Zeke asked.

"They run this camp, and every October, boys can go there for a long weekend," Harris explained.

"I've heard people talk about it for years. In fact, my dad went when he was a kid. And this year *I* finally get to go! We'll get to do all kinds of cool stuff—go canoeing, pitching a tent, and even telling scary stories at night!"

"And these things are fun?" Zeke asked.

Before Harris could answer, his best friend Roxy joined them on the bus.

"Well, you look pretty happy," she said to Harris.

"He is going to something called . . . Beaver Scout Camp," Zeke explained, still not quite sure what it was all about.

"So your parents finally think you're old enough to go? " asked Roxy. "Congratulations! I know how much you've looked forward to this. Is Zeke going, too?"

"No," replied Harris. *Actually, I don't think I know anyone who's going*, he thought to himself.

When the bus arrived at school, Harris pulled Zeke aside after they got off.

"Why don't you see if you can come with me to the camp?" he blurted out.

Even though he was excited, Harris was a little nervous about going off to camp and not knowing anyone else who'd be there.

"It'll be really fun, I promise, and a great way to learn about Earth kids!" said Harris.

"I guess it might be. . . ." said Zeke.
"I'll talk it over with my parents."

2 CAMPER ZEKE

THAT EVENING, ZEKE TOLD his parents about Beaver Scout Camp.

"Floating on the water? Sleeping in the outdoors? Scaring people with words? Why are these things fun?" asked his mom, Quar.

"I'm not really sure," Zeke admitted. "But Harris seems very excited about going. And he asked me to come along with him."

Zeke's dad, Xad, was happy that Zeke was fitting in here on Earth.

Each time he and Quar moved to a new planet, Zeke found it difficult to start over at a new school and make new friends.

"This could be a good thing, Zeke," Xad said. "You will learn more about how Earth kids behave. And it will really help our research!"

"I am a little concerned," said Quar. "Ever since you met him, Harris has been trying to prove that you are an alien. I'm afraid that spending so much time together might make it harder for you to keep our secret."

Zeke had decided not to tell his parents that Harris now knew the truth about Zeke being an alien. Zeke decided to trust him.

"I am not worried about that, Quar," Zeke said. "Harris apologized, and I think everyone was able to convince him that we aren't aliens."

"Okay, I guess it will be okay then," said Quar. "But be careful."

"I'm not sure I will have a good time doing all these strange Earth things," Zeke said. "But I do like the idea of spending time with Harris. Okay then, I'll go."

Zeke called Harris with the news.

"That's fantastic!" Harris cried. "We are going to have the best time ever!"

Well, I sure hope so, thought Zeke.

3 OFF TO CAMP

ON A CRISP OCTOBER MORNING, Zeke and his parents gathered with Harris and his parents in the driveway next to the Walkers' house. Roxy was also there to see them off.

"I believe that Zeke has all the necessary supplies," said Quar. "He has his emergency transmitter."

"It's called a cell phone," Zeke explained.

"And his nutrition-infusion packets," Quar continued.

"They're called energy bars," Zeke said.

"Oh, don't worry," said Harris's dad. "There's always plenty of food for the campers. When I went as a kid, we had a cookout every night!"

"I think it's so cool that you two are going together," said Roxy.

"Thanks, Roxy," said Zeke. "I wish you could come, too."

"Oh, don't worry about me," Roxy said. "I'm going to see a soccer game this weekend with my cousin Rebecca. You two just have a great time!"

"We will try," said Zeke.

"Well, don't make it sound like work," Harris said. "It's going to be fun!"

"Time to go," said Harris's mom. "We don't want to be late for the bus."

Zeke lifted a white, egg-shaped container from off his front lawn and placed it in the back of the car.

"What that?" Roxy asked.

"It's my travel pod," Zeke explained. "It holds my belongings."

"Oh, you mean your suitcase," said Harris.

Zeke, Harris, and Harris's parents climbed into the car and drove away.

"Bye!" yelled Roxy.

Zeke's parents waved. Harris thought they looked a little worried.

"Okay, let's make sure you have everything, Harris," said his mom. "Eight pairs of socks, right?"

"Yes, Mom."

"Five bathing suits, right?"

"Mom, we—"

"Three bottles each of sunscreen and bug spray, right?"

"Mom, we went over this four times in the house!" Harris said.

"I know, honey, but this is your first time away from home alone," said Mom.

"He'll be fine," said Harris's dad. "I remember all the wacky stuff I did when I was a camper. We had contests to see who could get their marshmallow the blackest and still be able to eat it. We stayed up all night on the trip playing games. Oh, and we climbed the tallest tree in the county. Wait until you get a load of this tree!"

A short while later, the car pulled into a parking lot. Kids streamed from their parents' cars and climbed on board the bus that would bring the campers to Beaver Scouts camp.

"Have a great time, Harris!" said his mom, hugging him. "You too, Zeke."

The boys grabbed their gear from the car and headed for the bus.

"I'm really glad you're coming with me, Zeke," Harris said, as the two boys stepped onto the bus.

4 ALL ABOARD

THE BUS WAS FILLED with a large group of laughing, screaming kids. Harris could feel the excitement.

For Zeke, the noisy bus reminded him of the sad feeling he had when he stepped onto the school bus just a few weeks earlier as the new kid at Jefferson Elementary School.

But the feeling passed. This time, he had a friend at his side.

As the bus pulled out of the parking lot, Patrick, the head counselor, stood up and got everyone's attention to be quiet.

"Welcome, Beaver Scouts!" he said with a big smile. "You are in for a great weekend! We'll be playing games and sports, going on an overnight camping trip in the woods, all kinds of totally cool stuff. Just sit back and relax, and we'll be there in a few hours."

Zeke looked out the window and watched the scenery change from large, family houses and shopping malls to scattered trees and farm fields. Soon, mountains came into view.

BANG!

A loud boom sounded and jolted the bus. It pulled over to the side of the road, then rumbled to a stop.

The driver and Patrick ran outside to investigate. A few seconds later, Patrick stuck his head back in as the driver grabbed a toolbox.

"Sit tight, everybody," he said. "We have a flat tire. I'll check it out."

"Oh, great!" moaned one boy. "Stuck here in the middle of nowhere!"

"What about this air pump?" Patrick asked the driver, pointing at it among the tools.

The driver shook his head.

"It's no good," said the driver. "There's a hole in the tire. I'll have to put on the spare tire, which will take a while. We're going to be late, I'm afraid." The two men got back on the bus to call the camp to let them know.

Zeke quietly got up and slipped out of the bus amid the commotion.

"Hey! Where are you going?" Harris followed, wondering what in the world Zeke was doing.

Outside, Harris watched Zeke kneel beside the flat tire. Zeke looked back toward the sky, and then he cupped his hands around the hole. Suddenly, they started to glow bright red.

"What are you doing?!" Harris whispered to Zeke, looking around, worried that someone might catch Zeke using his powers.

"I'm redirecting energy from the Earth's sun through my hands to heat the rubber enough so it'll melt and seal the hole in the tire," Zeke explained as casually as if he were telling Harris what he had brought for lunch.

A moment later, the bus driver stepped outside.

"What's going on out here?" he asked.

Zeke stood up.

"There is no longer a hole in the tire," Zeke explained. "You may now fill it using the air pump."

The driver knelt down and looked at the tire, astonished. Then he looked up at Zeke.

"He studied auto repair at his last school," Harris explained. "He's very talented."

The driver gave Zeke a funny look, then shrugged and pumped the tire full of air.

"You'll have to be careful this weekend around everyone," Harris whispered to Zeke when they got back to their seats. "We need to keep your secret safe!"

Zeke smiled. He was glad he had Harris to help him keep his secret.

BEAVER SCOUTS CAMP

THE BUS BOUNCED ALONG a bumpy country road surrounded by tall trees.

"Maybe that kid was right," Harris said to Zeke. "I think we really are in the middle of nowhere."

Zeke looked puzzled.

"How can anyone be nowhere?" he asked. "We are always, actually somewhere, wherever that may be."

Harris laughed. "That's true, but it's just an expression for a really far-away place."

The bus turned onto an even narrower, bumpier dirt road.

"I take it back," said Harris. "I think *this* is officially the middle of nowhere."

The bus rolled through a large entry gate. Above the gate swung an old wooden sign with the image of a beaver carved into it. The trees opened up into a clearing, and they passed a lake with a waterfall falling into it.

Harris got very excited. "I love being in the woods," he said.

Zeke looked puzzled again. "We have woods on Tragas, but nothing like this," he explained. "The trees are striped, the lakes are yellow, and the waterfalls flow *up*, not down."

The bus rolled to a stop in front of a flagpole in the center of a circle of cabins. Patrick stood up and spoke.

"Okay, listen up. They'll be four scouts to a cabin. Listen for your name and cabin assignment."

Patrick then read the names of all the campers and their cabin numbers.

"Cabin five—Harris, Zeke, Roger, and Paul," Patrick announced.

"That's us," said Harris, grabbing his backpack and heading off the bus.

Harris and Zeke walked into the spare wooden cabin. On either side were a pair of bunk beds. A few seconds later, two more boys came in.

"I'm Roger," said a tall, thin boy with red hair. "And this is my friend, Paul."

Harris recognized Paul as the kid who had complained about being in the middle of nowhere. Paul was short with curly brown hair.

"I'm Harris, and this is my friend, Zeke," said Harris.

Roger and Paul went to one of the bunk beds. Harris and Zeke walked over to the other.

"Would you prefer the top bed or the bottom?" Harris asked Zeke.

Without answering Harris's question, Zeke used his powers to float up into the top bunk.

"I guess that answers my question," Harris said. "I'm actually glad since I'm kind of afraid of heights."

"Whoa, how did you get up there so fast?" Paul asked from across the room. He pointed to Zeke, who sat on the top bunk.

"Zeke's a great climber," Harris said quickly. "You should see how fast he climbs up a rope!" Zeke laughed.

Roger smiled and nodded at Zeke. Paul narrowed his eyes, then went back to unpacking.

This Paul kid could be trouble, Harris thought. *Zeke will have to be extra careful around him.*

A whistle sounded from outside the cabin.

"Everyone to the flagpole!" Patrick shouted.

Camp was about to begin!

6

CANOE ADVENTURE

"OKAY, EVERYONE, LISTEN UP!" Patrick shouted as the campers gathered around. "In a few minutes, we'll head over to the mess hall for lunch."

"*Mess* hall?" Zeke whispered to Harris. "I've always been told not to make a mess with food."

Harris smiled. "It's just another word for the place where we eat," he explained.

Patrick continued. "After lunch, we'll meet at the river to teach you how to canoe and take a trip down the river. So . . . welcome to Beaver Scouts Camp!"

In the mess hall, Harris and Zeke sat with Roger and Paul.

"So, where are you guys from?" Roger asked.

"We both go to Jefferson Elementary School," Harris said quickly, hoping to avoid any talk about Zeke's true home.

"I'm originally from Tragas," said Zeke.

He really didn't have to say that! Harris thought.

"Tragas?" said Paul. "Where's that? Never even heard of it."

"It's pretty far from here," Zeke replied.

Harris quickly changed the subject. "I really like playing soccer," he said.

"Me too," said Roger. "I love soccer!"

But Paul eyed Zeke suspiciously.

After lunch, the campers all gathered at the river and began their canoe lessons.

Harris and Zeke put on their life vests and climbed into an available canoe. Roger and Paul got into another. They launched their canoes into the river. Harris paddled gently. They moved smoothly through the calm, flowing water.

"Hey!" Paul shouted from the canoe behind Harris and Zeke's. "How can they be that far ahead of us with only one kid paddling?"

Harris turned around and saw Zeke holding his paddle in his lap. But the water on either side of him was churning, pushing the canoe quickly down the river.

"You actually have to put your paddle in the water, Zeke!" Harris whispered. Then he shouted, "Paddle harder, Zeke!"

"Why?" Zeke asked Harris. "We move faster if I use mind projection to push the boat through the water."

"Do I have to remind you that you asked me to help you keep your powers a secret?" Harris asked softly.

Zeke sighed. "You're right," he said. "I will be more careful."

Zeke dipped his paddle into the river and moved it through the water. *Gosh, this is so much harder!* Zeke thought.

Roger and Paul slipped ahead of them.

"Hey, we're leading!" Roger said.

But Paul just glared at Zeke as they passed.

A short while later, the river split into two branches. To the right, it remained calm. But to the left, the water looked choppy and picked up speed very quickly.

"Everyone, steer right!" Patrick shouted.

But as they reached the fork, Roger and Paul had trouble steering their canoe. They were pulled to the left, into the fast, rushing current.

"Help!" Paul cried. "We went the wrong way!"

Roger panicked. He stood up in the canoe to try to get more power from his paddle, but he tumbled overboard into the churning, swirling current!

"Roger!" Paul screamed, looking down into the water.

RESCUE!

HARRIS WAS REALLY WORRIED. He saw Patrick paddling hard toward the spot where Roger had fallen in. Paul managed to grab an overhanging tree branch and pull his canoe safely to shore.

Harris felt his own boat suddenly zoom through the water back toward the fork. He turned and saw Zeke sitting quietly with his eyes closed. Their canoe cut through the rushing current like a motorboat.

Zeke is using his powers! Harris thought. *I hope he doesn't get caught, but he may be the only one who can get to Roger in time!*

When they reached the spot where Roger fell in, Zeke dove out of the canoe. He disappeared down into the bubbling water.

Harris paddled as hard as he could, fighting the current, and made it to the shore. He stared into the rushing water.

Come on! Come on! he thought.

Just as Patrick's canoe arrived, Zeke burst through the surface of the water with Roger in his arms. He helped Roger into the canoe, then climbed in after him. He and Patrick paddled hard to the riverbank as Zeke secretly moved their boat along using his powers.

Once they all got to shore, they carried their canoes over to the calm part of the river.

"You're quite a swimmer, Zeke," Patrick said once everyone was safely on shore.

Zeke looked puzzled. "I can't swim," he said, being completely serious.

Wow! Harris thought. *He must have used his floating power to move him through the water. So he wasn't actually swimming!*

Everyone laughed, thinking this was a joke.

"Thanks, Zeke," said Roger once he had caught his breath.

"Yeah, thanks for rescuing my friend," Paul added.

But Harris noticed a suspicious look on Paul's face, even as he was thanking Zeke.

After the canoe trip, the campers gathered for lunch.

"How are you feeling?" Harris asked Roger as they ate.

"Good as new, thanks to Zeke," Roger replied, patting Zeke on the back.

Zeke smiled. He felt like he had just made another human friend.

"Don't forget," Patrick announced as the campers finished lunch, "tomorrow we go on our overnight camp-out!"

ON THE WAY BACK TO THEIR
bunk, Harris explained to Zeke what
a campout was.

"Why would we sleep outside when
we have a perfectly fine bunk bed in
the cabin?" Zeke asked.

"Because it's fun!" Harris replied.

Zeke shrugged. "I guess it's just one more Earth thing I really don't understand."

The next morning, the campers gathered at the flagpole. They each had a backpack full of gear.

"Okay, campers. Remember, no cell phones or other devices," Patrick announced. "Leave them in your bunks. We are going into the great outdoors, back to a time before technology. Follow me!"

A line of campers followed Patrick onto a path that led deep into the woods. After hiking for about an hour, they came to a clearing. In the center was a fire pit made of stones.

"Okay, we made it! Wasn't that fun? Now we have to set up your tents in a circle around the fire pit," said Patrick.

Harris and Zeke pulled out their tent, placed it onto the ground, then crawled inside with the tent poles to set it up.

"I think that one goes over there, Zeke," said Harris, shoving a pole into the center of the tent.

Zeke stuck one end of a tent pole into the ground, then shoved the other end into a small pocket in the canvas flaps. But the pole popped out and poked Harris right in the butt.

Then the whole tent collapsed on top of them.

Both boys cracked up.

"Even though I've never done this before, I don't think we're doing it right," said Zeke.

Harris stuck his head out to see how the other campers were doing. Some were almost finished. Others, including Roger and Paul, were also struggling.

"You know, Zeke, no one is watching us," Harris said. "They're all busy trying to set up their own tents. So, um . . ."

Harris didn't have to finish his sentence. Zeke smiled and closed his eyes. He spread his hands wide apart, and the tent poles lifted into place perfectly. Then the canvas drifted down onto the poles until the tent was fully built and ready to use.

"You know, normally I would tell you to be more careful with your powers, but this was so much less annoying than building the thing piece by piece," Harris said. "I just hope no one noticed."

The boys crawled out from their tent to see Roger and Paul still struggling with theirs.

"Hey, how did you put that tent up so fast?" asked Paul, as a tent flap dropped down and covered his face.

"Camping is one of my favorite activities back in Tragas," Zeke said quickly. "I think it's so much fun to sleep outdoors 'in the middle of nowhere.'"

Harris turned away, afraid that if he looked Zeke in the eyes, he would crack up laughing.

When the sun went down, Patrick lit a roaring campfire. All the campers gathered around the blaze. They stuck hot dogs on sticks and roasted them over the fire.

After dinner, Patrick asked, "Who wants a marshmallow?" as he opened a huge bag.

Harris took a marshmallow, slid it onto a stick, and held it over the fire.

Zeke took a marshmallow from the bag. As he went to put it into his mouth, Harris noticed that the marshmallow was fully toasted.

"But you didn't even hold it over the fire first," Harris said, looking around to see if anyone else had also seen this.

"Why bother?" Zeke asked. "If the point is to heat the marshmallow, I can do that with my hands."

"But that takes all the fun out of it," Harris insisted.

"Fun like sleeping outdoors?" Zeke asked.

Harris laughed. *They just must have a different definition of fun on Tragas!* he thought.

The full moon rose above the blazing campfire.

"Kind of spooky out here, right? It feels like a perfect night for scary stories!" said Patrick.

"I've got a scary one," said Paul. Then he stood up and began.

9 SCARY TALES

BY THE FLICKERING GLOW of the campfire, Paul told the story of a brother and sister who were dared to go into an old, run-down shack in the woods near their town.

Kids in the nearby town thought it was haunted. Their parents told them that this wasn't true and that no one had lived there for decades, but the shack always seemed to have had a small, flickering light glowing inside of it. Whenever the kids walked by it, they always tried to get one another to knock on the door.

One night, the brother and sister finally took the dare. Deep in the dark, creepy woods, they found the vine-covered shack and knocked on the creaky door.

"It's open," said a raspy voice from inside.

The two kids looked at each other in shock, gulped, then opened the door and stepped into the shack. They pushed past cobwebs and sidestepped scurrying rats.

At the far end of the room in the dark sat a woman. Suddenly, she lit a candle, and in the light, they could see her warty, wrinkled skin. Her wispy white hair circled her head like smoke, and she smiled at them, revealing yellow, rotten teeth.

"Well, well," cackled the witch. "So nice of you to visit me. And, you're just in time for dinner. In fact, you're the main course! Ha-ha-ha-ha!"

The kids screamed and dashed from the house. As they ran through the woods, they could still hear the witch's hideous laughter.

They finally arrived at home, and burst through the front door.

"Mom! Dad! We're home!" they shouted, but then they stopped in their tracks.

There, standing in the hallway, was the witch!

"So, you've decided to have dinner at home," the witch said. "Excellent. In fact, I just finished eating my appetizers, though you know them as Mom and Dad!"

The door closed behind them, and they were never heard from again.

Paul finished and sat down. A few kids squirmed, and others laughed.

"I have a scary story, too," Zeke announced.

Harris was surprised, and a little worried.

Zeke stood up and launched into the story of the Kraka Beast of Tragas, a monster that eats trees and destroys buildings. Zeke told a tale of the destruction of an entire city by the beast.

83

"That's not as scary as my story," said Paul.

"Maybe, but mine is true!" said Zeke. Everyone laughed.

"So is mine!" said Paul jokingly.

"Forget it," whispered Harris. "*I* believe you."

The fire died down.

"Time to hit the hay," announced Paul. "Everyone go back to their tents."

Why would I want to hit hay? thought Zeke as they returned to their tents.

The next morning, the campers got up with the sunrise. They packed up their tents and started the hike back to the cabins. Along the way, Paul, Roger, Harris, and Zeke came to a stop at a very tall tree.

Paul pointed up at the tree. "You're supposed to be a good climber, right, Zeke?" he asked. "I bet I can climb that tree higher and faster than you or anybody else here."

"Not me," said Roger. "My mom's calling soon, so I have to get back to the cabin. See you guys back there." Roger continued along the trail. Harris looked up at the tree. *This must be the tree that Dad climbed when he was a camper,* he thought. *Only Dad isn't afraid of heights!*

10 THE CLIMB

ZEKE AND PAUL STARTED CLIMBING. They both moved quickly up the tree.

This would be so much easier if I could just use my powers, Zeke thought.

Harris really wanted to climb the tree, but he just couldn't seem to make himself walk over to it and begin.

Zeke glanced down and saw that Harris was still standing on the ground. He looked up at Paul, who was reaching for a branch high above him.

Zeke climbed back down.

"Let's climb together, okay?" Zeke asked.

Harris took a deep breath and stepped onto the lowest branch.

"Just go slowly, Harris," Zeke said. "I won't let anything happen to you."

Harris nodded and slowly made his way up the tree. He had only gotten a little way up when he heard Paul's voice from above.

"I beat both of you! Look at me!" Paul shouted from the highest branch. "I'm king of the tree!"

Paul raised his arms to the sky in victory, but somehow lost his balance and fell. He plunged toward the ground below.

"Aaahhh!" he cried.

Harris looked up helplessly and winced. There was nothing he could do to help.

Zeke closed his eyes and focused on Paul. He had to use his powers, but he couldn't be too obvious about it.

Zeke slowed Paul down a bit until he was just two feet from the ground, then he let Paul hit the ground at normal speed.

Climbing down quickly, Zeke and Harris rushed to Paul's side and helped him to his feet.

"Are you all right?" asked Harris.

"Yeah," said Paul, dazed. "It was weird. As I was falling, I felt like something was holding me, even slowing me down. I'm not sure exactly what happened. It's kind of a blur."

Then he paused, and looked right at Zeke. "Hey, um . . thanks," he said quietly.

"You're welcome," Zeke replied, flashing a sly smile. "But I'm not sure what you're thanking me for."

The following morning, the campers all boarded the bus for home.

"So what did you think of camp?" Harris asked Zeke during their ride.

"Interesting," Zeke said. "I still can't say that I understand humans that well, but I did actually have a good time with you."

When the bus arrived, Harris's parents were waiting for them, along with Roxy.

"How was it?" Roxy asked on the car ride home.

Zeke and Harris took turns telling stories about their adventures.

"Well, we're just glad that Harris got to go with a friend," said his mom.

"So," Roxy said, smiling. "See any aliens at camp?"

"Only this guy," Harris said, pointing at Zeke. Everyone laughed, believing that Harris was just kidding, making fun of himself for the way he used to think that Harris was an alien.

"Well," Zeke spoke up, "there *were* a couple of kids there that I wasn't too sure about!"

Harris smiled, happy that, at least for the moment, Zeke's secret was still safe.

Read on for a sneak peek at the fourth book in the Alien Next Door series!

THE ALIEN NEXT DOOR
TRICK OR CHEAT?
#4
illustrated by Anjan Sarkar
by A. I. Newton

HARRIS WALKER RUSHED NEXT DOOR to his friend Zeke's house. Harris and Zeke had only been home for a week following their adventure at Beaver Scouts camp, but already it felt like a million years ago. Halloween was coming this week, and that was all Harris could think about.

"Guess what?" Harris asked excitedly when he joined Zeke in his room. "It's almost Halloween!"

"Hall-o-what?" Zeke asked, repeating the unfamiliar word.

Harris smiled. He had become such good friends with Zeke that sometimes he forgot that his next door neighbor was not from Earth.

"They don't have Halloween on Tragas?!" Harris asked.

"Correct," said Zeke. "What is it?"

"Everyone dresses up in costumes," Harris explained. "For that one day, you can be whatever you want to be—a ghost, a monster, an animal, an object. Anything you can imagine! Then we all go out at night, trick-or-treating."

"What does that mean?" Zeke asked.

"We go from house to house and get candy," Harris said. "And the whole neighborhood is decorated with ghosts and cobwebs and other spooky stuff. Then we come home, watch scary movies, and eat our candy. It's the best holiday!"

Zeke looked puzzled. "So, once again, like when we were telling scary stories around the campfire on our scouting trip, we want to get scared because it's . . . fun?"

"Exactly!" Harris said. "Now you get it."

"I'm still not sure I do," Zeke said. "But I want to learn all I can about Earth culture. And I do appreciate you helping me make my way through your strange customs."

"Oh, and I almost forgot the best part," Harris continued. "Every year at school, we have a costume contest! All the kids and teachers dress up in Halloween costumes, and then the kids compete to see who has the best costume."

"I'm not sure why people would want to dress up in costumes," Zeke said. "But I do like competitions. Back on Tragas, we had contests to see who could levitate the heaviest load, or who could navigate a pebble through a bunch of moving rings."

"That sounds really cool! Do you know what you want your costume to be?" Harris asked.

Zeke smiled. "Well, If I understand you correctly about this costume contest, I don't think I need a costume at all," he said.

Harris was confused. "What do you mean?" he asked.

"I'll just go as . . . myself!" Zeke announced.